ONCE UPON A CLEAR, DARK NIGHT

D0095747

The Story of Christmas for Children
Based on Matthew 2:1–12

Written by Jeffrey E. Burkart
Illustrated by Natalia Vasquez

CONCORDIA PUBLISHING HOUSE · SAINT LOUIS

Once upon a clear, dark night,
A star burst forth with blazing light
That made all other stars look dim
As its light shined on Bethlehem.

And at that moment, there were those
Whose eyes up to the heavens rose.
They spied this star and wondered why
It had appeared up in the sky.

They said, "What is this strange new star
That shines so brightly from afar?"
"What can it mean?" "What should we do
That we might get a better view?"

One of those wise old scholars said,
"My friends, there's something I once read
About a city far away
Where kings are born, or so they say."

These learned men then made a pact:
They all decided they should act
And seek this king who was foretold
In ancient prophecy of old.

These wise men, who were called Magi,
Traveled as they watched the sky.
Over sands, through heat of day,
And through long nights they made their way.

Up to Jerusalem they went,
For every one of them was bent
On finding where this king might be
To solve this ancient mystery.

Straight to the palace they then sped
So they might find out from the head
Of government in this strange land
If he might lend to them a hand.

The horrid Herod, who was king,
Simply didn't know a thing
When they asked, "Do you have news
Of who is born king of the Jews?"

"Your Majesty, we've seen a light
That shined on us in darkest night
And points the way to one who'll be
The King who'll set all people free."

Then Herod on *his* wise men called
And each of them was so enthralled
By what the prophet Micah wrote
They went to Herod with this quote:

"O King, here is the prophecy:
'A king of Israel shall be
Born in the small Judean town
Of Bethlehem, where kings are found!'"

Then Herod called the Magi near
And asked, "When did this star appear?"
The Wise Men told him everything,
And Herod said, "Now, find this king!

"Go search in ancient Bethlehem,
It's just a few miles south, and when
You've found Him come right back, please do,
So I can come and worship too!"

The Magi left upon that day.
Led by the star, they found their way
Right to a house wherein they found
The child whom God alone had crowned.

They bowed their knees and gave Him praise,
And every Wise Man's voice was raised.
Then they presented Him right there
With gold and frankincense and myrrh.

And that night God warned them in dreams
Of all King Herod's wicked schemes.
For Herod sought to harm God's Son
Who came to save us, every one.

The Wise Men left and went back home,
And by another route did roam.
But they had found God's great surprise
When they looked in Jesus' eyes.

For those Wise Men saw the one
Who's God's one and only Son.
And all who in God's Son believe
The gift of God's new life receive.

Dear Parents,

And, lo, the star, which they saw in the east, went before them, till it came and stood over where the young child was. When they saw the star, they rejoiced with exceeding great joy. (Matthew 2:9–10 KJV)

The story of the Wise Men has developed largely from tradition. There are only a few solid biblical facts we can be sure of: the Magi, a group of distinguished, learned men, came from the East to worship the Christ Child. (Their identification as kings is linked to Isaiah 60:3, "Nations shall come to Your light, and kings to the brightness of Your rising.") And they brought with them three symbolic gifts: gold, frankincense, and myrrh.

Epiphany comes from a Greek word meaning "appearance" or "manifestation," and *Magi* comes from a Greek word meaning, roughly, "follower." Christians, followers of Christ, observe Epiphany on January 6 as the day that the Son of God was revealed to the Gentile world.

Have you ever had an epiphany? Has the light of understanding suddenly dawned on you? The idea of that kind of epiphany began with this Bible story. When you read this book to your child, you can talk about how we know that Jesus is God's Son and our Savior. It is a wisdom that comes from faith as a gift from the Holy Spirit. The Magi recognized the star as a sign of an ancient prophecy of the new King. Our knowledge of what God, in His overwhelming love, has done for us in sending His Son to the world is so much greater than that of the Magi. As you think about the star on your Christmas tree, you can rejoice that Jesus is that "bright morning star" (Revelation 22:16).

The Editor